Helen Orme taught as a Special Needs Co-ordinator in a large comprehensive school. At the last count she had written around 40 books, many for reluctant readers.

Helen runs writing workshops for children and courses for teachers in both primary and secondary schools.

Trouble with Teachers

Helen Orme

Rans☀m

Trouble with Teachers

by Helen Orme
Illustrated by Cathy Brett
Cover by Anna Torborg

Published by Ransom Publishing Ltd.
Rose Cottage, Howe Hill, Watlington, Oxon. OX49 5HB
www.ransom.co.uk

ISBN   978 184167 599 2

First published in 2007

Copyright © 2007 Ransom Publishing Ltd.

Illustrations copyright © 2007 Cathy Brett and Anna Torborg

A CIP catalogue record of this book is available from the British Library.

Meet the Sisters ...

Siti and her friends are really close. So close she calls them her Sisters. They've been mates for ever, and most of the time they are closer than her real family.

Siti is the leader – the one who always knows what to do – but Kelly, Lu, Donna and Rachel have their own lives to lead as well.

Still, there's no one you can talk to, no one you can rely on, like your best mates. Right?

To Angela

1

Book Week

It was nearly Book Week. The teachers had all sorts of things planned, but what was most exciting for Siti and her friends was the author visit.

A real writer was coming into school and she was going to be working with Siti's year group.

Mrs Williams told her English group.

"I want some volunteers to show Lola Leigh around. I need people I can trust."

Siti and the Sisters all wanted to be chosen.

The Sisters were Siti's best friends. They were really close and even their parents said

they were like sisters, so that's what they called themselves.

So many people wanted to help that Mrs Williams said she needed to think about it.

"I bet I won't be chosen," said Siti. "That's the trouble with having a dad who teaches

here. I never get chosen for anything in case people say it's because of him."

"I hope it's me," said Kelly. "I think I might be a writer."

Rachel snorted with laughter. "You! Your writing is awful. No one can read it!"

Kelly laughed. "It's not about handwriting, it's about ideas. That's what I want to talk about. I hope I get chosen."

2

Behaviour – and stuff

Next day Mrs Williams told the class what was to happen.

"Rachel and Lu will look after Ms Leigh," she announced. "I'll talk to you about it in a minute," she said, looking at Lu.

She turned to the rest of the class. "Now, remember – it's important that the author has a good time and goes away thinking that the school is a good one. You've got to be very well-behaved all day."

Siti stopped listening. She knew Mrs Williams would go on for ages about good behaviour. Siti was thinking about Kelly.

Kelly really did like writing, even if Rachel was right about other people reading it! She would have to do something to make sure that Kelly got a chance to talk to Lola. With Rachel and Lu as helpers, it should be easy.

"What did Mrs Williams say?" said Siti.

"Only the usual," said Lu. "The same as she said to the whole class really, about behaviour and stuff."

"She'll give us the timetable tomorrow morning," said Rachel. "We've got to show Lola where to go, carry her things and take messages."

"It'll be a good skive," said Lu. "We've got to go and meet her at the end of each lesson, even when she's not with our class."

"Good," said Siti, looking at Kelly. "We can get this sorted. Leave it to me."

3

Not you, Kelly!

They were at school early the next day, so Mrs Williams could tell them what to do. She gave the timetable to Rachel.

"I'll meet Lola. You can come to the staff-room at nine to take her to her first group. She's working with 9J. Meet her at the end and take her back to the staff-room for coffee."

The girls went off to their form room. Just before nine Rachel and Lu got up to go. So did Kelly.

"Not you, Kelly," said Mr Lester, their form tutor.

Kelly pulled a face.

"Never mind," said Siti. "We'll go with them at the end of break."

The class went off for their first lesson. Rachel and Lu were soon back.

"She's really nice," said Lu.

"She's with us after break," said Rachel. "We've got to change rooms. We're in the drama studio."

"That's miles away," said Siti. "What are we there for?"

"Dunno. We just are. But it does mean there's lots of time for Kelly to talk to her on the way."

4

Too shy

They were outside the staffroom just before the end of break. Rachel knocked on the door.

"We've come for Ms Leigh," she said.

The writer came out smiling.

"Hello, what a lot of people," she said, looking at the Sisters.

"These are our friends," said Rachel. "That's Siti, Donna and Kelly."

Kelly blushed and went very quiet.

"The drama studio's right over the other side of the school," said Donna. "So we thought we'd better come early."

Siti pushed Kelly towards Lola. "Talk to her," she said. But Kelly was suddenly too shy.

They walked down the corridor, with Lu leading the way and Rachel chatting to Lola.

They were just about to go out into the playground, which was the quickest way to get to the studio, when there was a sudden, terrible noise.

Siti looked out of the window. There was a big gang of year 8 boys milling around. She heard some very rude words!

"We'd better go this way," she said, pulling Lu in the other direction.

"What's the matter?" asked Rachel.

"Shush, year eights fighting," hissed Siti. "We've got to keep her away from them!"

They got to the cloakroom just as the bell rang. Everyone rushed in. The teachers were busy out in the playground dealing with the fight.

"We'd better wait a few minutes 'til the rush is over," said Lu.

It didn't take long. Everyone soon sorted themselves out and they were able to get through the doors. Unfortunately, now they were on the wrong side of the school.

Siti took charge. "Come on, this is the quickest way, round by the kitchens," she said.

The others followed but, as she went round the corner, she suddenly turned and blocked their way.

5

Not pleased!

Lola was beginning to look puzzled.

"Are you sure this is a good way?" she asked.

"Er, no," said Siti. "I think we'll go back through the playground.

Rachel sighed and led Lola back again.

"What's going on?" asked Donna.

"Two year tens kissing," said Siti. "We can't let her see them!"

When they got to the studio Mrs Williams was waiting outside. She did not look pleased!

She glared at the Sisters. "I'll see you all later," she said.

The lesson was great. Lola told them all about her work and, best of all, read to them from some of her books.

At the end everyone was really keen to start writing themselves.

Even Kelly got over her shyness.

"Where do you get your ideas?" she asked.

"Everywhere," said Lola. "I watch what people are doing and I listen to what they say, and that often gives me ideas for my books."

They were sorry when the bell went for lunch. Mrs Williams asked two of the boys to take Lola to the staffroom.

"I want a word with you five," she told the Sisters.

Lola smiled at them as she went out. "See you this afternoon," she said.

6

Another chance

"I thought she was never going to stop going on at us," said Rachel.

"It wasn't our fault," said Siti. "She told us we had to make sure Lola thinks this is a good school. She's not going to think that if she sees people fighting and kissing all over the place."

"Anyway, we mustn't mess up this afternoon," said Lu.

"You were lucky she gave you another chance," said Kelly.

Rachel and Lu went off to the staffroom to collect Lola. The rest of the Sisters went to their lesson. They had only just arrived when the other two got there.

"That was quick," said Donna.

"Yeah! We told Lola what happened and she said we'd better leave her and get back," said Rachel.

"She said we can all go back at the end of the afternoon and help her take her things to the car," added Lu.

They settled down to work.

Halfway through the lesson Mrs Williams came in. She was not happy!

She spoke to Ms Glynn and then called the Sisters outside.

"What do you think you're playing at? I expected better of you five."

They looked at her. "Sorry?" said Lu in a puzzled voice.

"So you should be. Why on earth did you lock Lola in the computer suite? You'd better come and say sorry. Now!"

7

Not their fault

The Sisters followed Mrs Williams to the staffroom. Lola was there. Laughing.

"I've found out how it happened," she said. "It wasn't their fault."

"9F had moved," she explained. "There was a problem with the computers so they had to find a new room. I didn't know so I sent the girls away and sat down to wait for the class. Then someone came and locked the door without seeing I was in there. I had

to wait until someone came past to get them to find a key and let me out."

"We're really sorry," said Rachel. "We were trying to be good," she added, looking at Mrs Williams.

"You were good," said Lola. "It wasn't your fault! You looked after me really well. In fact you've given me an idea for a new book."

"What's that?" asked Mrs Williams, looking interested instead of cross.

"A book about school."

"What will you call it?"

"Oh," Lola shrugged, "I don't know yet."

Later, as the Sisters walked out to her car, Lola grinned at them. "I've decided on a title," she said.

"What is it?" asked Kelly.

"It's going to be called 'Trouble with Teachers'!"